Uncle Phil's Diner

by Helena Clare Pittman

Carolrhoda Books, Inc./Minneapolis

Ladonne, who modeled for the
paintings of Ruthie.

Carolrhoda Books, Inc.
c/o The Lerner Publishing Group
241 First Avenue North
Minneapolis, MN 55401 U.S.A.

Website address: www.lernerbooks.com

LIBRARY OF CONGRESS CATALOGING-IN-
PUBLICATION DATA

Pittman, Helena Clare.
   Uncle Phil's diner / by Helena Clare Pittman
      p.   cm.
   Summary: Ruthie and her father play
games and share memories to keep warm
as they walk to Uncle Phil's diner on a
cold Sunday morning.
   ISBN 1-57505-083-8
   [1. Fathers and daughters—Fiction. 2.
Winter—Fiction. 3. Diners (Restaurants)—
Fiction.] I. Title.
PZ7.P689Un 1998
[E]—dc21   96-44326

Manufactured in the United States of America
1 2 3 4 5 6 - JR - 03 02 01 00 99 98

The wind is singing through the bare maple branches. They tap against my window, bobbing with fresh fallen snow. It's Sunday, and Papa and I are going to Uncle Phil's for breakfast.

I rush down the hall to wake him up, but the big bed is already made. I race downstairs and through the swinging kitchen door.

"Papa, are we going?"

"A little snow won't keep us home. But it's too cold to go in pajamas!" he teases.

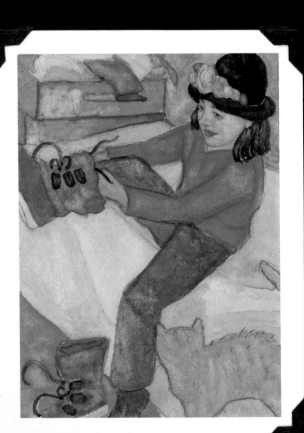

I gallop back up the stairs and nearly trip over Muffin, lacing through my legs.

"Two sweaters, Ruthie!" Mama calls from the kitchen.

I hurry to get dressed and put on my galoshes.

Muffin sniffs the cold wind at the door. She's happy to be staying home.

Mama wraps a wool scarf around my neck. "Keep warm!" she says, hugging me. "Send my love to Phil and Ida and the girls!"

At last Papa and I start down the street. The diner is ten blocks away.

Uncle Phil gets up before the sun, no matter what the weather is like. He walks through the quiet streets, past brick buildings and blue morning shadows.

He climbs the wooden steps to the plank boardwalk above the sand. He passes a row of stores and unlocks the door of Number 33. Then he sets to work making breakfast. His hungry regulars will be there soon.

Our street looks neat and new under fresh snow. On Mr. Jacobs's front porch, a fat newspaper flaps in the wind. Suddenly it's lifted by an icy gust. Its pages scatter, waltzing against the sky. Papa and I gather them up and tuck them under the milk box.

But the wind is too bitter for us to stop for long. It presses against us as we walk. I turn up my collar and try to keep my teeth from chattering.

"Think warm, Ruthie!" says Papa.

"Do you think Uncle Phil is making the blueberry pancakes yet, Papa?" I ask.

"Stacks of them!" he answers.

I imagine my uncle's pancakes sizzling on the black iron griddle. He's wearing the apron Aunt Ida has starched and ironed. I can see him stirring flour and milk and eggs together in a big bowl.

Big enough for all Uncle Phil's customers—Mr. and Mrs. Berman, Mr. Pukatch, Mrs. Raphael. Big enough for Papa and me.

The best part of the pancakes are the blueberries—preserved at the summer cabin in the mountains.

"Papa, remember how hot it was the day we put up the blueberries with Aunt Ida?"

"It was so hot we could hardly move!" answers Papa.

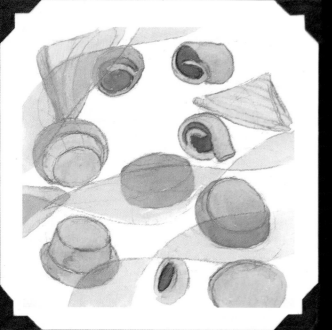

"It must be almost as hot in Uncle Phil's kitchen!" I think of the smell of rolls steaming in the tall, black oven, and Uncle Phil's rugelach and apple strudel, turnovers and muffins and sugar buns.

"Buns and muffins, cookies and bread," I sing.

"Pancakes and syrup, cupcakes and cocoa," answers Papa.

Our singing makes clouds of steam. For a little while I feel warmer. Then I'm shivering again, and the boardwalk seems like the other side of the world. "I'm freezing, Papa!"

"Think warm, Ruthie!" says Papa.

plow
a path for
   White
ns line
walk.
s make
as we
e street.

"Papa, my legs
are tired!"
"Sharp turn
ahead! Hold on!"
cries Papa, taking
my hand. At the
end of his arm, I
ski around the
corner and slide
past darkened

At the train station, we stop in to buy a newspaper. Down the tracks, a light grows brighter and brighter. Finally a train pulls into the station, pushing a cloud of warm air. Pigeons huddled on the rafters coo happily.

Papa tucks his newspaper under his arm, and we step back into the cold. "Four more blocks!" he announces.

We come to a smooth, white lot between apartment houses. I make a snow angel. Brrr! I shiver from cold, wet snow that creeps beneath my gloves.

For a moment I lie, gazing up at the sky. I imagine the people who sit in the shade there on hot, humid days, fanning themselves to keep cool. Now their laughter mixes with the winter wind.

At the cabin, I lie under the stars with my cousins Millie and Nettie. We listen to the crickets singing in the warm, sweaty night and sing in harmony.

Papa and I cross the avenue to the park. The swings and slide are covered with snow. The benches are piled with drifts.

"Biscuits and butter!"
Papa sings to keep warm.
  "Rolls and jam!" I answer.
  "Buns and muffins!"
  "Pancakes and pie!"
  "Uncle Phil's pancakes
are piling up," Papa
reminds me. "Let's hurry!"
  Our legs sink into the
snowdrifts. The wind
snaps. I don't think I'll
ever feel warm again.
"Papa, it's too cold!"
  "Think warm," answers
Papa.

Suddenly the beach stretches just

The street ends, and we step onto the snow-covered sand. The cold ocean water makes the wind even colder. "Remember when we had a picnic here last August, Ruthie? It was so hot, not even the ocean could move!"

My father's words melt the snow. I remember the feel of hot sand between my toes. My cousins and I are splashing in the water, trying to stay cool.

Papa lies buried in the sand.

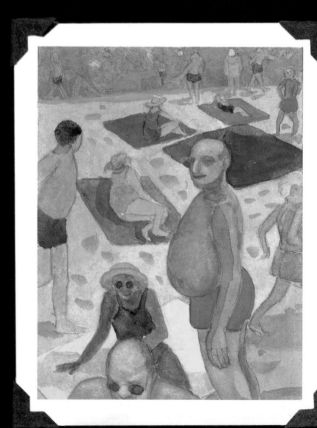

People of all sizes and shapes cover the beach.

The whole Pincus family is there, everyone in their bathing suits.

Except Grandpa.
"Papa, this isn't the old country," says my mother. "Are you going swimming in a suit and tie?"

I trudge after my father over the snowy dunes. Wild waves slap the shore. Papa waits for me, huddled against the wind. "Papa, you're shivering!" I tell him when I catch up.

"It is cold, Ruthie," he says softly.

"Just think warm, Papa!" I remind him, and he chuckles.

For a moment, the wind dies. The beach grows silent.
We listen to the water, watching the snow fall.

Suddenly we hear bells. "Listen!" Papa whispers.
A sanding truck turns the corner, its wheels wrapped in
jingling chains.

Papa looks at me and smiles. There's frost on his glasses and ice on his eyebrows. His cheeks are glowing. Then he points. "Look, Ruthie, there's an oasis ahead!"

"**Phil's Diner**" is blinking from the boardwalk, coloring the snow neon pink. We climb the steps to Number 33.

Warm air greets us as we open the door. Mr. Pukatch nods, and Mr. and Mrs. Berman smile over their steaming coffee.

Mrs. Raphael warms my cold face with her hands. "Such beautiful rosy cheeks, Ruthie!" she exclaims.

The table is set for Papa and me. Uncle Phil serves us a platter of pancakes.

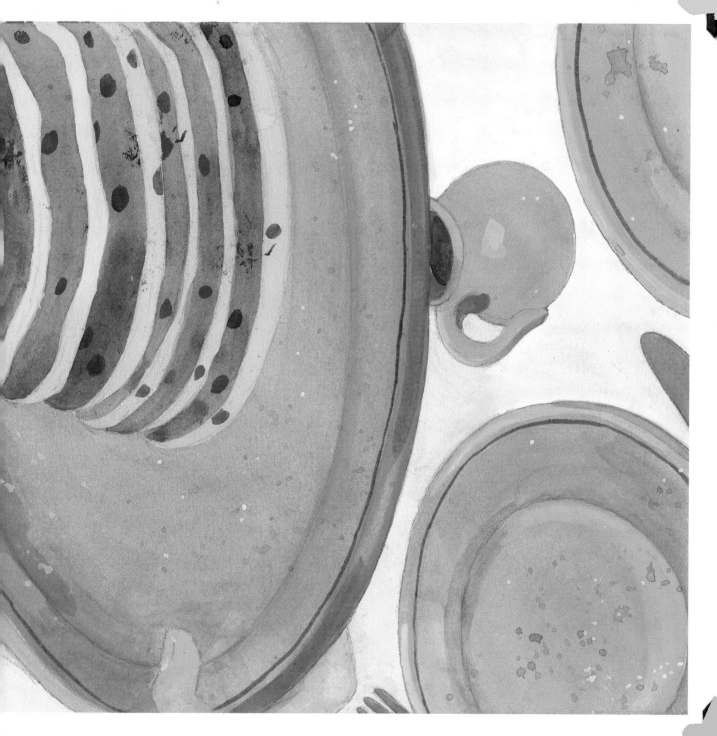

The pancakes are sticky and sweet with syrup. Hot cocoa works its way down to warm my toes. We eat until we're stuffed. Then Papa reads the newspaper and talks with Uncle Phil.

I help my cousins Millie and Nettie in the kitchen.

As Papa and I are putting on our coats, Aunt Ida arrives to prepare lunch. She won't let us leave until she fills a bag with fresh-baked treats to bring to Mama.

We close the door, leaving the warmth of the diner behind us. Papa takes my hand, and we start home. The wind off the waves is still icy. But Papa and I are warm, stuffed with blueberry pancakes.

"Buns and muffins, biscuits and bread!" I sing.

"Cakes and cookies, doughnuts and pie!" Papa answers back.

Recipe for **Uncle Phil's Blueberry Pancakes**

1½ cups sifted flour	2 tablespoons melted
3 teaspoons baking powder	margarine or oil
½ teaspoon salt	¾ cup blueberry preserves or
2 eggs, beaten	1 cup fresh, canned, or
1 cup milk	frozen blueberries, drained

Combine flour, baking powder, and salt in a mixing bowl. Add eggs, milk, and margarine or oil. Stir just until moistened. Gently mix in blueberries. Do not overmix. Heat ½ tablespoon oil or margarine in griddle over medium heat. (Be sure to ask a grown-up for help before you heat the griddle.) Using a ⅓-cup measure, drop batter onto hot griddle. When batter rises and bubbles appear around edges, turn pancakes and cook until the undersides are golden and the centers are no longer doughy. Serve with maple or blueberry syrup. Makes 8 to 10 4- to 5-inch pancakes. Mm-mmm-mm!

For my daughter, Theo: Together we walked so often in the cold, playing games to keep ourselves warm.

HCP 1997

And for my cousins, Nettie and Millie, and their parents, Aunt Ida and Uncle Philip, in remembrance of times that now live inside us and bind us to one another, outside of time.

$15.95

DATE			